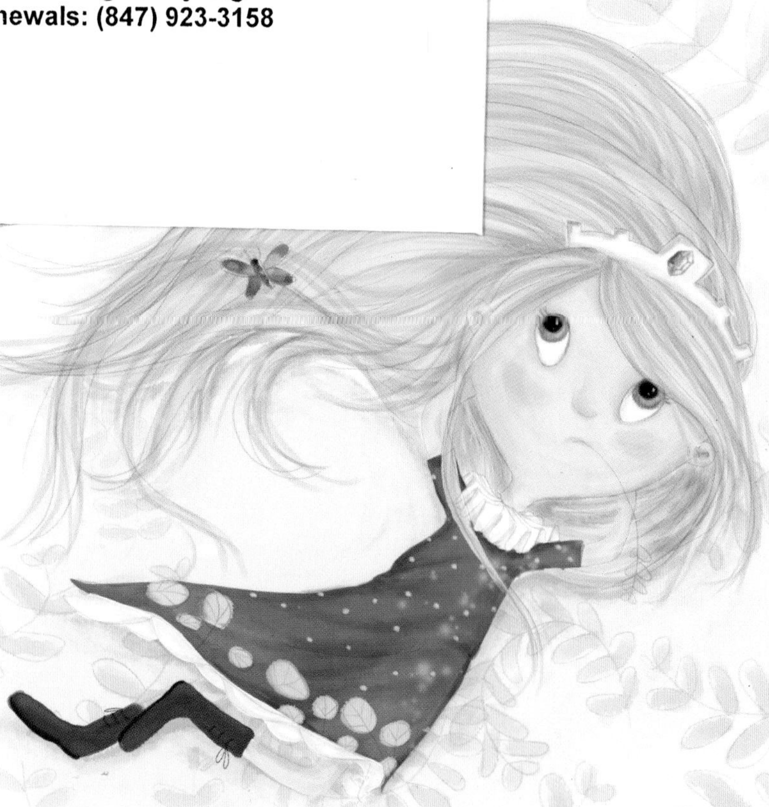

Princess Lila
Builds a Tower

By **Anne Paradis**
Illustrated by **Karina Dupuis**

This is Princess Lila.
Princess Lila had everything
she needed to be happy.

She lived in an enormous castle
in a land where the sun shone every day.

Princess Lila's bedroom was like something from a fairy tale.

The shelves of her bookcase bent under the weight of many books.

Her toy box overflowed with toys.

Her closet could barely contain all of her beautiful dresses.

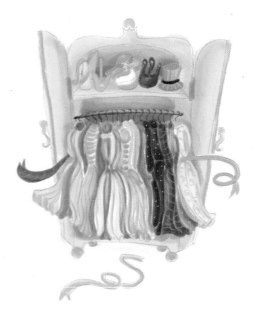

Princess Lila had many servants whose only task
was to take care of her.
Some of them were in charge of her education,
and others brushed her hair
or prepared her favorite foods.

Yes, Princess Lila really did have everything to be happy.
Yet she was bored.
She wanted to see what lay beyond the forest
that surrounded the castle
and discover the entire country.
She wanted to meet people from other places
and play with children her own age.

Her parents were very firm:
Lila was not allowed to venture into the forest.

"The forest is teeming with fierce and cunning animals.
It's much too dangerous for a princess!"
"Lila dear, you can do absolutely anything you want,
but you can't wander around in the forest."
Princess Lila had to stay inside the castle walls.

For a long time, Princess Lila had been trying to find a way to see over the trees that circled the castle. She made stilts. She climbed ladders. She reached for the sky on her swing.
But no matter what she did, the dense leaves of the forest stopped her from seeing the horizon.

One day during her drawing lesson, her tutor asked her, "Princess Lila, what would you like to draw today? A cat? A rosebush? A little butterfly?"

"I want to draw plans for a tower. A tower higher than the castle. Higher than the trees in the forest."

The teacher clapped his hands with glee.

"Ah, a project worthy of my talents! Architecture, geometry, mathematics …"

Princess Lila interrupted him.

"I don't want to just draw a tower. I also want to build it so that I may climb to the top and see all the way to the horizon."

The teacher tried to stay calm.

"Of course, Princess Lila. As long as you don't go into the forest, Your Highness can do anything you like."

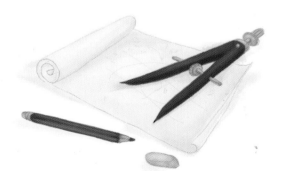

Princess Lila and her teacher spent hours at the drawing table.
They sketched and calculated, traced and erased and started over.

When the drawings were ready, Princess Lila's parents approved the plans.
"Lila dear, what a wonderful idea! We appoint you construction manager." Princess Lila blushed with happiness.

At last, construction of the observation tower
could begin. The teacher took charge of gathering
the materials, and Princess Lila gave all of the
castle workers new duties.

"Mr. Carpenter, you will put up the frame."
"The cooks will make the mortar, and the pastry chefs will lay the bricks."
"Ms. Hairdresser, you will weave a sturdy rope."
So, every castle worker had a job on Princess Lila's construction project.

As Princess Lila's dream was about to come true, she became more determined than ever. She got up early every morning to open the construction site. All day long, she supplied the workers with encouragements and refreshments. She even did some of the work herself.

The hardworking princess was always the last one to put down her tools. She would sleep a few hours and start all over again the next day.

Princess Lila's energy was contagious. The building
began to seem like an enchanted castle.
The observation tower grew higher every day.
Finally, after several weeks of work, the tower rose
above the treetops.

The people who lived in the castle were invited to a big party to celebrate the official opening of the tower. Lila's parents thanked the workers and congratulated their little girl.

"This is for you, construction manager: a spyglass to let you see very, very far away." Princess Lila hugged her parents.

"Your dream is about to come true, Lila dear, may you discover the world and all its treasures."

And they opened the tower door for her.

Princess Lila began to climb the spiral stairway. She was so excited that her heart pounded. It seemed to take forever to get to the top. She had to stop often to catch her breath.
At last, Princess Lila reached the very top of the tower. She took a deep breath and stepped onto the observation deck.

What a beautiful sight! The treetops went on as far as she could see. Princess Lila looked through her spyglass for a better view of the horizon.

On one side, she could see the dark blue sea. On the other, she spotted a herd of deer in a clearing, and farther away, a hilltop.

Next to it, Princess Lila
saw a castle like her own,
with a wall and a high tower.
She looked carefully all
around it and then she saw
a child like herself.

Princess Lila smiled and waved.
From the far side of the forest, a boy waved back to her.
Princess Lila had a friend. Now, she truly had everything she needed to be happy.

CrackBoom! Books is an imprint of Chouette Publishing (1987) Inc.

Text: Anne Paradis
All rights reserved.
Illustrations: Karina Dupuis

Chouette Publishing would like to thank the Government of Canada and SODEC
for their financial support.

Canada

Québec
Books
Tax Credit
Gestion
SODEC

Bibliothèque et Archives nationales du Québec and Library and Archives Canada
cataloguing in publication

Paradis, Anne, 1972-
[Princesse Lila et le château en chantier. English]

Princess Lila builds a tower

(CrackBoom! Books)
Translation of: Princesse Lila et le château en chantier.
For children aged 3 and up.

ISBN 978-2-9815807-5-7

I. Dupuis, Karina, 1982-   . II. Title. III. Title: Princesse Lila et le château en
chantier. English.

PS8631.A713P7413 2017   jC843'.6   C2016-941702-6
PS9631.A713P7413 2017

CRACKBOOM! BOOKS

©2017 Chouette Publishing (1987) Inc.
1001 Lenoir St., Suite B-338
Montreal, Quebec H4C 2Z6 Canada
crackboombooks.com

Printed in Malaysia
10 9 8 7 6 5 4 3 2 1 CHO1993 JAN2017